Collywobble

Malachy Doyle

Illustrated by Petra Brown

Pont

For Juno

First published in 2012 by Pont Books, an imprint of
Gomer Press, Llandysul, Ceredigion, SA44 4JL

ISBN 978 1 84851 320 4

A CIP record for this title is available from the British Library.

© Copyright text: Malachy Doyle, 2012
www.malachydoyle.com
© Copyright illustrations: Petra Brown, 2012

Malachy Doyle and Petra Brown have asserted their moral right under the
Copyright, Designs and Patents Act, 1988
to be identified respectively as author and illustrator of this work.

This book is published with the financial support of the
Welsh Books Council.

Printed and bound in Wales at Gomer Press, Llandysul, Ceredigion

Farmer Joe's sheepdog had seven pups.

Three were big and strong.

Three were good enough.

But one was the most shivery little scrap
you've ever seen.

'What a wobbly collie!' said Farmer Joe, as the
tiniest pup tried to stand up for the very first time.
'Hey, that's what I'll call you – Collywobble!'

The three big strong ones went off to be sheepdogs.

The other three went off to be pets.

But nobody chose Collywobble – he was just too small.

'You can stay here with me, I suppose,' Farmer Joe told him one morning. 'But you'll have to earn your keep!'

Next day the snow
began to fall.
   'We'd better go and fetch
the sheep down from the hill,'
said Farmer Joe to Collywobble's mum,
Bess. 'You mind the place while we're away!'
he told the little pup, with a laugh.

But by two o'clock there was no sign of them,
and Collywobble was getting hungry.

By three o'clock he was worried.

And by four o'clock it was getting dark.

Collywobble set off up the lane to see if he could find them.

The snow was freezing cold on his tiny paws, and every now and then he'd sink in till he was nearly buried.

'Baaaaa!' A great army of sheep was coming down the lane towards him. The nervous little pup hid in the snow and waited for the truck, with Bess and Joe inside, to appear.

But there was still no sign of them. Where could they have got to?

The sheep marched right on into
the farmyard, and suddenly
Collywobble knew what to do.

He ran and pushed the gate tight shut to keep
them all safe inside. Then he raced off up the lane.

What was that? Was it his mum barking?
'Help!' she was saying. 'Help! Help!'

Collywobble ran down the bank and . . .

. . . there was Farmer Joe's truck, on its side
in the snow – with Joe and Bess trapped inside!

Collywobble took off up the track, as fast as he could go . . .

. . . till he reached Farmer Dai's house.

'You're Joe's little pup, aren't you?' said Dai.
'Have you gone and got lost in the snow?
Here, hop in my truck and I'll take you home
before the weather gets any worse.'

But when they got to the bend where Joe had skidded off the road, Collywobble yapped and yapped.

'What's the matter, boy?' said Farmer Dai. And then he spotted the broken fence, and the tyre marks in the snow.

'Goodness me!' said Farmer Dai when he saw
what had happened. He helped Joe and Bess out
of the crumpled truck, and back up to his own.

'You've a clever little pup there, Joe,'
said Farmer Dai. 'You'd have been in
big trouble without him!'

Now Collywobble's mum, Bess, is the wobbly one, till her leg's better.

And Farmer Joe's a bit wobbly too, after his bang on the head. So guess who's doing all the hard work around the farm?

Collywobble!

Because he's not a wobbly little scrap of a thing any more. He's a proper working sheepdog, and he's brave as brave can be!

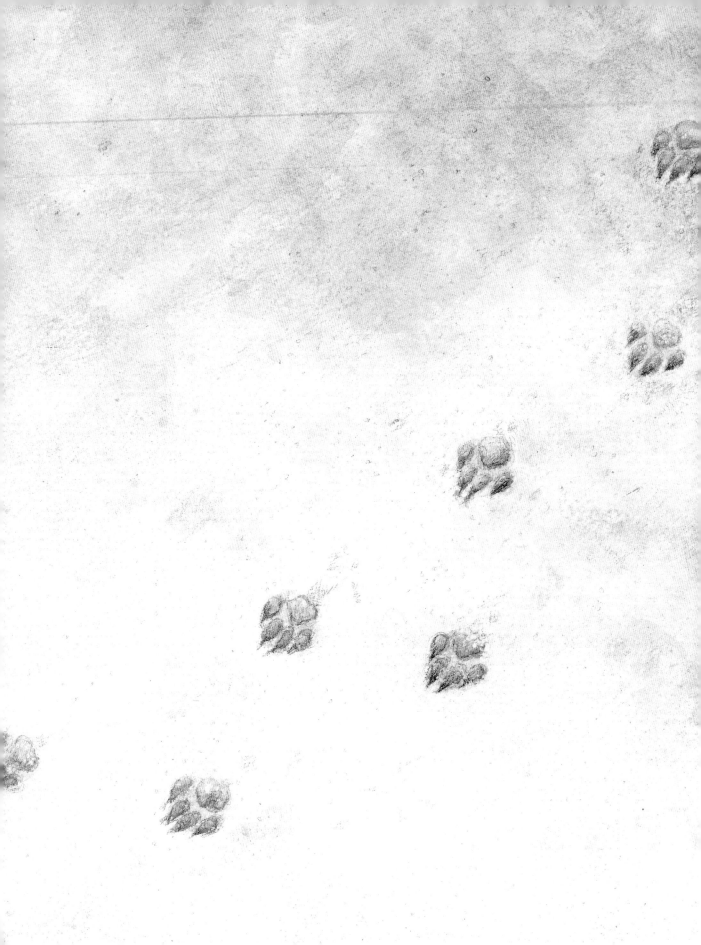